D1151530

FEATHERLIGHT

PETER BUNZL

Illustrated by
ANNELI BRAY

Kensington and Chelsea Libraries

3 0116 02113790 4

For Paula

First published in 2021 in Great Britain by
Barrington Stoke Ltd
18 Walker Street, Edinburgh, EH3 7LP

www.barringtonstoke.co.uk

Text © 2021 Peter Bunzl
Illustrations © 2021 Anneli Bray
Chapter heading illustration © 2021 Evan Hollingdale

The moral right of Peter Bunzl and Anneli Bray to be
identified as the author and illustrator of this work has been
asserted in accordance with the Copyright, Designs and
Patents Act, 1988

All rights reserved. No part of this publication may be
reproduced in whole or in any part in any form without the
written permission of the publisher

A CIP catalogue record for this book is available
from the British Library upon request

ISBN: 978-1-78112-918-0

Printed by Hussar Books, Poland

CONTENTS

1

AFTER MIDNIGHT

Mum shakes me awake in the middle of the night. She is sitting on the end of my bed and her face looks worried. Outside my window, the light from the lighthouse sweeps across the bay.

"Mum," I ask. "What's the matter?"

"The baby's coming early, Deryn," Mum replies. "I have to go to the mainland and get help."

Mum sounds scared. Panic makes my chest feel all spiky.

"I need you to fetch your father," Mum says to me.

I scramble to my feet and put on my slippers. My hand shakes as I light the oil lamp at my bedside. A book of fairy tales I was reading before I went to sleep slips from the table. It falls to the floor with a loud crash.

Mum picks the book up and shuts it. "Hurry!" she cries.

I leave her and race out. The rooms in our cottage are dark and silent. The only sounds I can hear are the creak of the wind on the roof tiles and the wash of waves in the distance.

I push open the door that leads to the lighthouse. The stone walls inside curve around in a circle. A thick pipe sprouts from the floor to the top of the tower, taking oil from the tanks in the cellar up to the light.

I climb the spiral stairs, holding the lamp in front of me, and open the door at the top.

This is the keeper's office. My favourite room in the lighthouse. The pipe runs right up into here. Beside the pipe is a writing desk and a curved bookcase full of books on the sea, ships, tides, flags, stars and nature. Books about the birds and animals that live on our island. They contain everything you need to know to be a lighthouse keeper.

My dad is sitting in his armchair, writing in his red logbook. His lantern, flask of tea and telescope are on the table beside him. A fire crackles in the grate of the stove by Dad's feet. He's been up here all night, keeping an eye on the ocean and checking on the lantern light upstairs. It's the most important part of his job. The light from the lighthouse keeps people at sea safe.

"What is it, Deryn?" Dad asks when he sees me.

"It's Mum," I say. "She needs you."

And Dad knows exactly what I mean.

"Come on," he says, standing up and taking his coat from the back of the door.

2

A NIGHT-TIME GOODBYE

In the cottage, Dad finds Mum's leather bag, which she has already packed in preparation for this day. Then Mum, Dad and I set out across the island towards the jetty.

It is a Sunday night in late October and there are no boats in the bay. Every few seconds, the lighthouse beam sweeps across us. Dad links his arm with Mum's, while I walk ahead. I'm carrying Dad's lantern so we can see our way along the path in the dark when the flashing light is facing the other way.

We are the only people who live on this island, and the lighthouse and cottage are the only buildings here. The sea around us is filled with rocks that are as sharp as swords. As sharp as your worst worries.

Those rocks are hidden beneath the waves. They can sinks ships and take your life. They have killed many people in the past, and they will cut you to shreds if you let them. That's why the lighthouse is here, to warn of those dangers.

But Mum and Dad will be all right in our small boat. Dad is a good sailor and knows how to navigate in the dark. And tonight the sea is calm.

Soon the jetty and the boat are in view. Gentle waves lap against the stony beach and the boat's hull. Dad steps down into the boat, and I pass him the lantern.

Mum hugs me goodbye. I put my hand on her belly, which is as round as a ball. The baby kicks beneath my palm and Mum winces.

"I will miss you," I say.

"I won't be gone long, Deryn," Mum says.
She's smiling, but her eyes are full of worry.

"Why don't you let me come along?" I blurt out. "I could look after you."

This will be my first time alone on the island. I haven't ever been away from my parents before, and they have never been away from me.

"I'll be fine," Mum tells me. She wipes a wisp of hair from my face and kisses my cheek. "We're going to stay with Grandma, like I did when you were born. Your dad will fetch the midwife, and she and Grandma will both be there to help me during the birth."

"What about me?" I ask. "What should I do?"

"You've got the most important job," Mum says. "You must stay here and take care of the lighthouse until we get back."

"When will that be?"

"Tomorrow," Dad says. "As soon as Mum's had the baby. You'll be fine to make your way home in the dark, won't you, Deryn?"

I nod. "I have the light to guide me," I tell Dad.

"Good," he says. He sounds a bit unsure. "Keep the watch, and promise me you'll do your school work and chores in the morning. I don't want you spending the day running around the island chasing sea birds!"

"I promise," I say.

"By the time you're done with that, we should be back," Mum adds. She takes Dad's hand, and he helps her down into the boat.

I untie the moorings, while Dad mans the tiller and the bowline.

"Goodbye and good luck, Deryn, darling!" Mum calls out, her voice cracking with worry. "You be good!"

"You too!" I shout as the boat sails off. "See you soon!"

I watch the boat get smaller. Fear flaps inside me like a ragged sail in a storm. The tiny lantern on the boat's prow floats like a firefly in the darkness as Dad steers between the rocks. The next time I see Mum she will have a baby in her arms. That's if things go well.

From their worried looks, I'm not so sure they will.

3

MY SHOOTING STAR

When I get home, I climb the stairs to the
lantern room at the top of the lighthouse, above
the keeper's office.

There always has to be someone watching
the sea and the lantern in case of emergencies.
For the rest of the hours of this strange night,
that person has to be me. For the first time
ever, I am by myself in the lighthouse, taking
Dad's place on the night watch. That scares me
a little.

Up here, the walls are made from glass
panels. That way the light beam from the oil
lantern can pass through them in the dark.

The lantern itself is not that big, but it's surrounded by lenses and a silver reflector and a metal stand and machinery that take up almost the whole room.

The machinery and stand help the lenses to rotate. The lenses have blackout sections that make the light flash every three seconds.

The flashing is important – it helps the ships far out at sea work out which lighthouse they are seeing, where they are on their map and how close they are to the rocks.

That way the sailors can keep themselves safe.

I check the oil reservoir beneath the lamp. It is getting low, so I pump the pump handle. The pipe gurgles as it sucks oil from the tank in the basement and spits it into the lamp's reservoir. Now there should be enough oil to keep the flame burning until morning.

Next I turn the big wheel on the wall. This winds the clockwork that keeps the lenses of the lantern turning.

Dad normally does both these jobs, but they're my duty tonight. It's hard work as the pump handle and the wheel are both very stiff. I have to summon all my strength to get them moving.

Outside the tower, the light beam revolves and the stars twinkle in the dark. It feels like the loneliest spot in the whole world up here, and I feel like the loneliest girl in it. I wish I wasn't on my own. At least Mum and Dad have each other.

I imagine them on the silent sea, looking up at the lighthouse and the same stars as I can see. I think of them heading for the mainland to have the baby. Filled with fear but sailing the ocean together. I picture the full moon and our light beam shining bright above Mum and Dad to light their way.

I try not to think of all the things that could go wrong for them. Instead, I list in my head the names of the star constellations that Dad has taught me: the scorpion, the wolf, the crow, the phoenix—

Just then, I see something ...

A streak of orange glittering in the dark.

A shooting star.

Its tail burns bright behind it, like a fiery red comet.

The shooting star lands somewhere on the far side of the island.

I shut my eyes and the shooting star sparkles in my memory.

It is my shooting star.

Tomorrow, I will go and look for it, but right now, I need to go down to the keeper's office and take Dad's seat for the watch.

*

I know I'm not meant to, but at some point during the long night I fall asleep. The chair is so comfy and the fire so warming, and I am so tired that I just can't keep my eyes open.

I dream that I climb the stairs again to the top of the tower. This time I step out onto the gallery, a metal walkway that runs around the outside of the lantern room. I breathe in the fresh sea air.

The full moon is tinted a fiery red and the sky is peppered with shooting stars. The light beam flashes past me. I look into Dad's telescope, watching the stars falling, and my hair grows longer and longer. Soon it is cascading over the edge of the walkway and down the side of the tower, just like Rapunzel's.

In my dream, my hair carries on growing until it reaches the bottom of the ocean, where a tiny baby swims in the dark.

The baby grabs hold of my hair and begins to climb up. My head hurts as it takes the baby's weight. It is so heavy that every strand of hair feels as if it might be ripped away as the baby climbs.

The baby carries a small stone. It climbs all the way up the side of the lighthouse to the walkway. There, the baby reaches out a fist and drops the stone into my hand.

The stone is actually an egg. Cracks appear in the egg's surface, and red light spills out, brighter than the light beam. So bright it almost blinds me. The egg breaks open and inside is a golden feather that burns me like the sun.

4

THE LIGHTHOUSE

I wake and look around me, feeling cold and tired. It is morning and I am in the keeper's office. For a moment I wonder what I am doing here, sitting in Dad's armchair. Then I notice that the fire in the stove has gone out.

A jolt of guilt zips through me. I must have fallen asleep on watch. Dad told me never to do that!

I jump to my feet and rush upstairs to the lantern room to check everything is all right. Daylight floods the glass windows, but the lenses still turn and the lamplight still flickers. The light has been working for the whole night.

Relieved, I put out the flame and stop the clockwork.

Outside the day is calm. The sea is quiet with only a few ships passing. There's no sign of trouble. No water-babies, or eggs, or burning feathers ... Did I really dream all that? Then I remember what really happened – the shooting star and how I vowed to find it. Mum and Dad setting off for the mainland because their real baby was about to be born.

That's why I'm up here alone. I promised Mum and Dad I'd look after the lighthouse. That means I'm no longer the lighthouse keeper's daughter. I'm the lighthouse keeper!

At least until they get back. I wonder when that will be. Has Mum had the baby yet? Do I have a little brother or sister? If so, I hope he or she is all right.

When Dad and Mum get back, they'll expect to find the chores done. That's a lot of work for one person to do on their own. Especially someone as young as me. I should probably get started on the chores before I look for my shooting star. Dad and Mum will be cross if they come back this afternoon and find that nothing has been done.

I wipe the lantern lenses with a cloth. This is the first job Dad does every day. It cleans the soot off the lenses and stops the lamp from clouding up and weakening the light. When I have finished that, I head downstairs to the empty keeper's cottage to make a start on the rest of the chores.

5

COMPLETING THE CHORES

It's strange to be here in the lighthouse keeper's cottage on my own. But I am used to doing chores for Mum and Dad, especially in last few weeks. Mum's been so ill during the final stage of her pregnancy that she's barely left her bed. I've had to help Dad around the lighthouse much more than I used to, so I know what has to be done.

I step into the yard and wash my sooty hands with water from the hand pump. Then I go to the shed on the far side of the house. I milk the goat, whose name is Gertrude. I collect the eggs from our three chickens, Bertha, Brenda and Bella, who live in the hutch next door. When I am finished, I have half a pail of milk and three eggs.

In the kitchen, a bowl full of dough rests on the table, beneath a tea cloth. Mum made it last night for the morning and left it out to rise. The dough has grown immensely and bulges from the bowl. Beneath the cloth it seems as big and round as Mum's belly. The fire in the stove has turned to ash. I build it up with logs from the basket, wait for the flames to get good and hot, then put the dough on a tray in the oven.

While the dough is baking into bread, I heat some water in the kettle for tea and some more in a pan to make myself a boiled egg.

I sit down to breakfast and flick through my school books. Dad and I have been reading *A History of Astronomy*. I decide I will look up shooting stars and see what the book has to say about them:

Shooting stars are meteors: the trails of rocks falling from outer space. The light that you see from a shooting star is the meteor burning up in the sky as it passes through Earth's atmosphere. When a meteor lands on the Earth, it is called a meteorite. A meteorite may look like a big shard of black rock.

By the time I've eaten my egg, the kitchen is filled with the warm and sweet smell of the baking bread.

I take the loaf from the oven. You are supposed to wait for it to cool. Mum always does. But I'm still hungry.

I cut off a steaming hunk of bread and stuff that in my mouth for my second breakfast. Then I cut another steaming hunk and stuff that into my cardigan pocket for my lunch. Finally I close *A History of Astronomy* and set off across the island to look for my meteorite.

6

AROUND THE ISLAND

Our island is called Featherstone Island because the ragged rocky coastline makes it look like a feather. There are no trees. It's too windy and wild for them to grow. The only tall thing is the lighthouse. It is the sort of tower you might imagine a princess from a fairy tale living in, except it's painted with red and white stripes so it can be seen far out at sea.

Featherstone Island is very flat and tufted with grass. The earth is rich with seabird droppings, and the grass is straight and strong. On the side of the island closest to the mainland we grow vegetables in the sheltered patches in our walled allotment. There are pumpkins and squashes that are nearly ready for cutting, and carrots ready to lift. Sometimes we fish off the rocks with lines and nets, and other times we collect cockles and mussels to eat.

The sea and sky change all the time here. In spring the sea can be so flat and blue that you can't tell where the water ends and the sky begins. In summer the clouds sit on the horizon like floating herds of sheep. In autumn the thunderhead clouds are as big as mountains and as black as the ink in Dad's inkwell. In winter it rains most days and the waves get so rough they look like sheets billowing from a clothes line on a windy day.

You might imagine it would be lonely being an only child on a small island, but there are all sorts of creatures to study and play with.

As well as our goat and hens, there are wild rabbits and sea birds – cormorants, divers, gulls, terns and skimmers. Sometimes there are seals and sea lions, even dolphins. Occasionally I have

seen whales surfacing to blow water far out at
sea.

And there are all sorts of fish: fish for
catching and fish for eating, and fish just
for watching in rock pools. Plus crabs and
barnacles. If you love wildlife like I do, then
Featherstone Island is the perfect place to live.

Truth be told, I have never lived anywhere
else. Twelve years ago, Mum went to the
mainland to have me with Grandma's help.
While she was away, Grandpa came to work
with Dad on the island. He had been the
lighthouse keeper before, when Dad was a boy.
Grandpa taught Dad everything he knows, just
like Dad is teaching me.

Gulls screech and circle above my head. The
sea crashes on the shore in its non-stop rhythm
as I walk around the rocky edges of the island
searching for my meteorite.

I look everywhere, but there's nothing to be found.

By the time I am done it is late in the afternoon. Mum and Dad still aren't back from the mainland with my baby brother or sister. I realise then with a shiver that I will be spending another night on the island alone.

7

LIGHTING THE LANTERN

It is almost evening when I fill Dad's flask with warm milky tea. I cut off another big hunk of bread from the loaf for dinner and put it in my pocket. After that, I take a hot water bottle, an oil lamp, matches and a blanket up to the keeper's office in preparation for the night watch.

In the office, I lay out my provisions on the desk. Then I climb the stairs to the lantern room, where I open the glass door of the lantern and light the lamp wick so the flame will already be burning when it gets dark.

I close the glass door and pump the pump handle beneath the lantern to fill the oil reservoir, just like I did last night. Once that's done I turn the big wheel on the far wall to wind the clockwork. When I've finished, the machinery beneath the lantern begins to tick and the lenses on their frame start to spin in front of the light.

Soon, when it's dark, the turning beam of light will reach far out to sea once more, warning ships away from the rocks. Not that they will need it tonight, for the sea is once again calm and clear.

I step onto the metal walkway outside the lantern room and stare at the distant mainland. I wonder how Mum and Dad are doing over there. I hope they're all right. I hope Mum's had the baby.

THUD!

Something smacks against the glass beside me.

The noise is so loud it makes me jump. And again ...

THUD!

I turn to see a bird about the size of a sparrow battering against the window.

Birds do that sometimes – hit the glass of the lantern room.

But this is unlike any bird I've seen before. Its chest is scarlet, like a robin's, and its wings are dirty red. It has a bright orange crest on top of its head that looks like the flames of a fire.

To tell the truth, this bird doesn't look well. A bit mangy. And it's small – it must have only recently been a chick. Perhaps it has only just learned to fly? If so, it isn't very good at it.

THUD!

The bird throws itself against the glass for a third time. It seems to be attracted to the light. Finally, it gives up and drops to the floor of the walkway, tired.

I crouch beside it. The bird shifts and tries to flap away from me. Then it opens its mouth to give a desperate cry.

"Hello!" I whisper to it. "Don't worry. I'm not going to hurt you. I'm here to help."

The bird licks its pale-grey beak with a darting tongue. It watches me with intelligent eyes that are as dark as wet pebbles. It seems to know exactly what I am thinking. The bird flaps its wings again and a warm breeze wafts off them like a ray of desert sunshine.

Close now, I notice some of the bird's feathers are damaged. Maybe it has been in a fire? It needs my help to get better. I can see that. Gulls scream above us in the evening sky. If I don't take the bird inside soon, they will be down here to eat it.

I wonder what the bird eats. Tomorrow, when the sun rises, I will show it our garden and try to find out. That's if I can get it to come with me now.

Making myself brave, I hold out my hands to the bird, hoping it won't try to peck my fingers off. When it doesn't flinch, I bend forward slowly and scoop the bird up.

I put the bird in the pocket of my cardigan, where it will be warm and safe, and then I climb back into the lantern room of the lighthouse.

8

A LOST BIRD

Back in the lighthouse keeper's office, I fold up my blanket to make a little nest for the bird. Huddled in the blanket, it looks tiny and helpless.

I tear off a corner of my bread and offer it to the bird.

The bird doesn't take any.

I pour some tea from my flask into an empty saucer on Dad's desk and push that towards the bird instead.

"Go on," I say. "Try the tea. It's good. Nice and milky. I put in three teaspoons of sugar.

It's more than I'm allowed when Mum and Dad are here."

I dip the bread in the saucer of tea, but the bird turns its beak up at that too. I've never met such a fussy creature.

"What kind of bird are you?" I wonder aloud. I take Dad's bird book down off the shelf and flick through the pages to see if I can find out.

It is a beautiful book, full of colourful birds of all kinds: puffins, terns, seagulls, cormorants, crows. Males, females and chicks. But nothing looks like my bird. I can't find it anywhere.

"If you're an undiscovered species," I tell the bird, "they'll have to name you after me. You'll be the Deryn Bird, and so will all of your kind!"

The bird looks at me sternly from its nest.

"Never mind," I tell it. "I shall give you a name that's just for you."

I have thought a lot about names recently, because Mum and Dad keep making lists of names for the baby. If it's a boy, they want to name him Albert, after my grandfather. If it's a girl, they want to name her Ida, after my great aunt. I suggested Cyrus for a boy and Grace for a girl, but they weren't sure about either of those. Names are hard. It took me ages to name the chickens.

The bird is pretty small. I think it might be a girl. I shall give it a girl's name.

"I shall call you Tan," I tell the bird. "Do you like that?"

She looks concerned.

"Oh, don't worry," I say. "It's not a name I suggested for the baby, so there's no chance you'll both have it."

Tan makes a tiny chirrup at this. She seems happy with her name. I realise I haven't told her about the baby. Or anyone else, really. There's been no one to tell. I've had to keep my worries and hopes all to myself.

9

AN UNEXPECTED ARRIVAL

Despite how tired I am, I manage to stay up for the whole watch that night. Somehow, having Tan there keeps me awake. I do doze off a couple of times, but when I wake I always remember to check on the lantern.

Twice during the night, I have to fill the oil reserve with the pump and wind the wheel to keep the lenses turning. It's only when the sun rises that I sit in Dad's chair and finally fall properly asleep.

I dream I am snoozing in my own bed with Tan beside me on my pillow.

For some reason in my dream the room is on fire. Soon the whole cottage is burning. Flames leap around me until Mum and Dad appear. They are ghostly figures, floating in the grey smoke as if they are underwater.

Dad shakes me, trying to wake me from my slumber, but I'm so tired I can't get out of bed. "Deryn!" Dad cries. "Wake up! You're on fire!"

"You're burning!" Mum adds, flapping her arms in the air like wings as she tries to put out the flames.

Mum and Dad make several loud *CAWING* noises, like seagulls, and Dad sweeps the lamp from the bedside table with a *CRASH*!

I wake in the keeper's office.

It is midday and the *CAWS* are coming from the seagulls outside the window.

But something is burning … for real! I can smell it!

Part of Tan's nest is on fire. She has knocked over the oil lamp. The last dribble of burning oil must have flooded on to her blanket and set it alight.

I use my cardigan as a glove and quickly set the oil lamp upright. Luckily its glass chimney isn't broken. Then I pour the rest of the flask of cold milky tea over the flames to put them out.

A horrible smoky smell fills the room. Tan opens her mouth and gives a low cough. But she is all right. She was tucked up on the other side of the nest, unharmed. The lump of bread is still beside her. Tan hasn't eaten any of it in the night, which can't be a good thing. But, anyway, somehow this morning her feathers seem brighter.

With relief I pick Tan up and put her back in my cardigan pocket. She curls up comfortably in there, warming my side.

Now that I am properly awake I climb the stairs to the lantern room and put out the flame of the big lantern also. When I've finished, I go down to see Brenda, Bertha and Bella in their hutch and Gertrude in her shed.

Between them, the three hens have laid only one egg today. Gertrude headbutts me angrily and refuses to be milked, so I decide to leave her until later.

Provisions are getting low. I hope that Dad returns today with more food. Otherwise I will have to forage for cockles and mussels along the coast.

Before I have my breakfast, I decide I will try to find something for Tan to eat. I wander out into the walled allotment garden, where we grow all our vegetables. I take Tan from my pocket and put her down beside a large orange pumpkin that has yet to ripen. Then I find a spade and start to dig in the raised bed. The earth is damp and soft. I turn it over, looking for worms and grubs. Part of this is to teach Tan to feed herself.

Each time I find a worm, I put it down next to her.

"Here you go!" I whisper. "Juicy worms!"

Tan doesn't seem interested. She ignores the long slimy creatures.

I stare at her, frustrated. "Worms are what you're supposed to eat, you stupid bird!"

Why doesn't Tan want them? Is she still unwell?

I glance up for a second, thinking. Then, all of a sudden, I see something in the distance.

A figure.

Someone is walking slowly up the path from the jetty and across the island towards the lighthouse. Even at this distance I can tell it isn't Mum or Dad.

"Deryn!" the figure calls out as it gets closer.

It's Grandma. As soon as she gets near enough, she grabs me and hugs me tight.

"There's good news and bad news," Grandma says, and my heart twists in my chest like a fish on a line.

10

GRANDMA DARLING

I sit at the kitchen table, beside the stove. Tan is curled up once again in my cardigan pocket. I check on her intermittently.

Grandma potters about the kitchen. She spoons tea leaves into the teapot and pours in hot water from the kettle on the stove. She is making herself busy, preparing to speak. She knows the house well from the years she used to live here when Grandpa was alive. Back then she was the assistant lighthouse keeper.

Soon the tea is ready. Grandma pours out two cups of tea from the pot, then sits beside me and clears her throat. I place my hands around my tea cup, letting the warm feel of it comfort me while I wait warily for the news.

"Your mother's had the baby," Grandma says. "It's a little boy. But there were complications. And your brother, he's not very well."

I don't really know what that means. It sounds scary.

"Have you seen him?" I ask, my heart beating a bit too fast.

Grandma doesn't answer at first. Then she says, "I don't want to worry you, Deryn. Everything's going to be fine, I'm sure."

"But where are they?" I ask.

"Safely tucked away at my house," Grandma says. "The midwife's keeping an eye on them. Your dad's staying too. He asked me to sail over here and look in on you. I can stay for as long as you need me."

"Thank you," I say, and put my hand in the pocket of my cardigan to stroke Tan's soft feathers. Somehow the warm feel of them soothes the worry away. Maybe if I can look after Tan and make her well again that will mean the midwife can help my baby brother.

"What have you got there?" Grandma asks. She has seen me fidgeting.

"A little bird that crashed into the lighthouse," I say, opening my pocket to show her. "I named her Tan. I'm looking after her until she's better."

"How nice." Grandma smiles. "I used to tell your father when he was small: 'A lighthouse keeper is not just here to tend the light and save ships. We're here to take care of the birds and beasts of the island too.' You're doing a fine job at that, Deryn."

*

The rest of the morning, Grandma and I clean the lighthouse together. Grandma says it's to get it ready for my parents' return, but I think it's because she feels it's got a bit scruffy since she lived here.

"When you're worried and waiting," Grandma says, "it's best to find things to take your mind off your troubles. Like your bird, Deryn, and tidying the lighthouse. It will be nice for your parents to come back and find everything here spick and span and shipshape!"

While we work, Grandma tells me stories about when she and Grandpa used to live at the lighthouse with Dad. "Your dad was such a naughty boy," she says. "He was always chasing Gertrude into the kitchen."

"You had the same goat?" I ask, shocked. "Gertrude doesn't look that old."

"It was a different goat," Grandma explains. "It just ... well ... our goats have always been called Gertrude. Your father continued that tradition."

"Oh," I say. "I see."

Names again. I think of Tan, and then of the baby.

"Have they named my brother yet?" I ask.

"I'm not sure," Grandma says. "There's so much else going on that I don't think your mum and dad have decided ..." She trails off, looking worried once more, then changes the subject. "I'll tell you something, my bunions are itching like billy-o today. That means there's bad weather on the way. Now autumn's here, the storms will be coming more often."

After we've cleaned the cottage, the last thing we do is polish the panes of glass in the lantern room. I forgot to do it this morning. As

we clean them, I explain to Tan how the light works. Grandma listens. She finishes buffing the panes on her side of the lantern first, and comes over to inspect how I am doing.

"You've missed a spot," Grandma says, pointing out a cloudy section. "You're talking too much to that bird."

I crouch down and clean away the last of the soot. As I do, I realise I have barely said anything to Grandma. Not for the whole afternoon. Not since she first arrived and told me how ill my brother was.

11

BEDTIME STORIES

That night, Grandma and I set the lighthouse light going together. Afterwards, Grandma brings me down to bed and, when I'm in my pyjamas, she tucks me in.

"I'll take the night watch tonight, Deryn," Grandma says as Tan settles beside me on the pillow. "But you can take the tea." She puts Dad's flask on my bedside table.

"Thank you, Grandma," I say.

"Do you want me to read to you?" Grandma asks. "I know your mum normally does." She takes the book of myths and fairy tales from my bedside and flicks through it. She finds a story near the back that I have never seen before. "Ooh, this is good one," Grandma says. "It was your father's favourite. I used to read it to him when he was a boy."

"What's it called?" I ask.

"*The Firebird*." Grandma reads the opening paragraph. "Tales are told of lost sailors who befriend firebirds. The firebirds would drink the oil from the sailors' lamps and then fly above their ships, lighting the way for them. Nowadays, no one has ever seen a real firebird. They disappeared thousands of years ago and only exist in ancient legends—"

"Stop," I say, and shake my head. "I don't think I can listen to a fairy tale tonight. There's too much to worry about."

"All right." Grandma closes the book and puts it aside. "Maybe I could tell you a story about something else instead?" she suggests.

"Like what?" I ask.

"Did you ever hear about the storm of '53 when a fishing trawler smashed against the Featherstone Rocks?"

I shake my head.

"It was the worst storm I ever saw," Grandma says. "The gale was so bad that the whole lighthouse shook. The floors moved, and the shelves rattled. And your grandpa and I had to go out in the dark in his rowing boat and save a whole host of sailors from that trawler before it sank."

"Were you scared?" I ask.

"A little bit," Grandma says. "But I knew we were their only hope, and if we could rescue the sailors and get them back to the lighthouse, then they'd be fine."

"Did you?"

"Yes, we did," Grandma tells me.

"And did they survive?"

"Every last one of them. They were safe here." Grandma leans in close to me. "This lighthouse is wise in many ways, Deryn. The walls are thick, and the stones know the weather as well as we do. They know when to be strong, and when to bend and shift to survive a storm. And the walls know the wind could never blow this house down, no matter how much it huffs and puffs."

Grandma kisses my forehead. "Time to go to sleep now. I'll be up in the tower, keeping an eye on the light. But if you need me, just come and find me."

"Goodnight, Grandma," I tell her as she's leaving. "I'll see you in the morning."

"That you will," she says, and she leaves the door ajar on her way out.

When she's gone, I say goodnight to Tan, but the little bird is already asleep.

12

A WILD STORM

That night I dream that Tan escapes from my room and flies through the cottage.

Grandma has left the door to the lighthouse open, and Tan flaps inside and flies down to the cellar. I chase after her, and she lands on the oil tank. The lid of the oil tank is open, and Tan dips her head in and takes a drink, guzzling down the oil as if it's water.

"Tan!" I cry. "What are you doing? That will kill you!"

But Tan ignores me and keeps on drinking. As she does, her feathers get glossier, her coal-black eyes glisten and her plumage starts to glow. Soon Tan has turned a radiant golden red. She is shining like a tiny dot of pure light, like she might burst into flame. Suddenly, I realise what she is.

"You're a phoenix, Tan," I say in my dream. "A firebird!"

Tan nods, and the light from her feathers seems to pulse with the brightness of that truth.

Then someone cries, "Wake up!"

*

Grandma is shaking me. The walls of my room are shaking too. And the bookshelf. And the glass of water on my bedside table. Rain clatters on the roof, and the wind howls outside my window. It feels like the storm in Grandma's story. Or like a wolf the size of the world is trying to blow our house down.

"The lantern, Deryn!" Grandma cries. "The lighthouse lantern's gone out! There's no more oil in the tank! There's a fishing boat out there in the gale, getting pulled towards the rocks! We have to warn it! We have to re-light the lamp! Is there any spare oil anywhere?"

Grandma picks up the lamp by my bedside and shakes it, but its reservoir is empty. She puts it back down in despair. "Think, Deryn!" Grandma says. "We need to make light!"

Then I remember my dream. I look around for Tan, but she's gone.

"Oh no!" I say. "I've lost Tan!"

"The little bird?" Grandma asks. "Don't worry about her just now. We have to find a way to get the lamp lit."

I nod. But I have a horrible feeling that I know exactly where Tan is.

"I think my bird might be able to help us, Grandma," I say.

"How?" she asks, confused.

"Trust me."

Grandma grumbles, but she lets me take her hand and we rush down to the cellar.

There is Tan, sitting on the edge of the empty oil tank. She's shining as bright as day, just like in my dream. My mouth drops open. The dream was true.

"Tan," I say. "You really are a firebird!"

Grandma looks at Tan and then at me, utterly shocked. "How on earth?" she says.

"Remember the story, Grandma?" I say. "About the firebirds who would drink the oil and light up the route for lost sailors?"

"That's just a fairy tale, Deryn," Grandma says. "It can't possibly be true!"

"It is!" I say.

I hold out my hands for Tan, and she flaps over to them.

I cup her in my palms. Tan is not hot, but her light is so powerful it pours over my fingers like water, making the skin of my hands glow bright orange.

"Look!" I say. "Look how brightly Tan is shining! Maybe she can light up the lighthouse lantern?"

Grandma looks amazed, but she is quick to regain her composure. "Do you really think Tan will be strong enough to light the way?" she asks hesitantly.

"There's nothing else to try," I reply. "There's no more oil in the house, and we have to help those people in that boat!"

Grandma still looks unsure, but she knows that this is our only chance.

"All right," she agrees, finally. "I can't believe this is happening, but I hope it works!"

Light spills from Tan and out of my hands as Grandma and I run from the cellar up the winding spiral stairs.

On each floor we pass, I see the fishing boat out of the window, struggling in the wild storm. It is being dragged closer and closer to the rocks.

"We must hurry!" Grandma says. "We need to warn them off before their boat gets broken apart!"

13

A BRIGHT HOPE

By the time we get to the top of the tower, the fire in Tan's feathers has died away somewhat. She almost looks like a normal small bird again. But she is still glowing softly, so that we can see the room.

Rain clatters on the tin roof of the lighthouse as Grandma and I open the glass door to the lantern and place Tan inside. I peer at Tan in the half-light. She stands on the metal surround of the lamp wick like it is a perch and blinks at us as if she's waiting for something.

"Please," I say to Tan. "Light up! Light up bright enough to flood the sky. We have to save the people on that boat!"

But Tan does nothing.

I feel sick.

"It's not working, Grandma," I say.

"I did warn you, Deryn," Grandma says. "The things you read in story books aren't always true."

But I'm not ready to give up just yet. I look at Tan. "Please, Tan," I beg. "There are people out there who are going to die unless we help them. Please light up and save their lives."

And it is as if Tan has understood me, for the light of her feathers grows stronger with each word. By the time I finish speaking, Tan is all afire, burning with the brightest blaze I have ever seen.

I cover my eyes as the glass lenses beam Tan's bright light out across the sea towards the distant boat. Grandma squints and shuts the glass door of the lantern. She turns the wheel beneath it to wind the clockwork, and soon the lenses begin to spin.

We run onto the metal walkway outside the lantern room. Grandma takes the spyglass from her pocket and snaps it out into a long telescope. She peers into the eyepiece, sweeping the spyglass across the ocean, searching for the boat.

"There they are," Grandma calls out above the noise of the storm. "I can see them ... And it looks as if they can see the light! Thank goodness! The boat is moving away from the rocks. I think they're going to be all right."

"Let me see!" I cry.

Grandma hands me the spyglass, and I focus in on the tiny fishing boat. There are three people aboard it: two fishermen and a boy. They're all trying to hold the tiller and control the sail, but the wind is pulling them in the wrong direction. With an almighty *CRASH!* they smash against the rocks.

"It's no use," I say. "They're going to drown."

"Then we must row out and save them," Grandma tells me as we climb back inside.

"We don't have a lantern to guide us," I say.

"We'll take your firebird," Grandma replies.

I shake my head. "What about the lighthouse?" I ask. "If we take Tan, then the light will go dark again. Other boats might need it!"

"My goodness!" Grandma wrings her hands together. "I didn't think of that, but we must take Tan anyway. She's the best thing to keep us safe."

"Wait," I say. "I have an idea."

I shield my eyes from the light and open the door to the lantern. "Tan, you must come with us. There's a boat in trouble. But I need to ask a favour of you. I need to take a feather. Will that be all right?"

Tan nods as if to say yes. She turns and plucks a feather from her tail carefully and gives it to me.

I take the feather by its stem. It is aflame but not hot. I place it in the centre of the lantern.

Tan flaps from her perch and circles my head, her feathers all ablaze. She gives a loud cry that sounds like an alarm call and swoops down the spiral staircase. We follow her, leaving the single burning feather behind in the lighthouse lantern to take Tan's place.

14

A RESCUE

The rain outside is falling like a waterfall. It hisses against Tan's bright flaming feathers as she hangs in the air, riding the air currents and lighting up the land. The raindrops batter down on my head and Grandma's, and onto our raincoats, which we struggled into as we left the house. But we can't stop. We have to get to the sinking boat and save the two fishermen and the boy.

Tan circles above us, lighting our way as we cross the island.

At the jetty, Grandma's boat is bouncing on the wild sea, thrown this way and that by the storm.

We climb down into the boat as high waves break over the side. I pull out the telescope and once again search for the fishermen. Tan soars up high, throwing her light out to sea. It joins the weaker beam of light from the feather in the lighthouse tower.

Finally, I see the remains of the boat. The two fishermen and the boy are clinging to its broken hull as angry waves smash against them.

"Fly ahead, Tan!" I cry, while Grandma releases our boat from its mooring. "We're counting on you to light the way!"

Tan swoops up into the sky, cutting a path through the rain and gusts of wind.

It is too dangerous for us to raise our sail in such a storm, so we row out into the bay towards the sinking boat. Grandma is on one oar and I have the other. We pull with all of our might, fighting against the waves and the wind and the rain, which are trying to smash us against the rocks.

At last we get close to the overturned boat. Tan is hovering above it, marking its position. In the glow of her light, I can see the two fishermen and the boy bobbing about in the waves. They are trying desperately to keep their heads above the water. Their faces are pale with worry.

The boy kicks towards us first. Without thinking, I reach out my hand to yank him over the side to safety.

"No!" Grandma screams above the pounding waves. "Not that way! He's too heavy. He'll capsize our boat! Over the back! Pull him in over the back!"

Grandma grabs my oar from me and sculls the boat around so the stern is facing the boy. Then she and I take a hand each and drag him into our boat.

The boy splutters and coughs. Water is streaming down his face and clothes. He brushes his hair from his eyes and turns around, looking for the other two fishermen. They are already kicking towards us.

The boy helps us haul them both aboard, one at a time. The older fisherman hugs the other two, then turns to us. "Thank you!" he says. "Thank you for saving my sons! And thank you for saving me! We can help you row!"

The fisherman and his elder son take an oar each. Grandma and I and the young boy sit in the stern while the two men row. Grandma shouts instructions over the storm, and Tan hovers above us, lighting the way.

Finally we reach the jetty. The prow of our boat smashes into it with a shudder.

I leap out and help the others onto the island one by one. I look for Tan. Without her, we would never have found our way around the dangerous rocks.

Tan drifts slowly down towards me. Her light is fading. She falls the last few metres to the ground. I can barely make out her dim shape in the dark. I scoop Tan up and hold her in my hands, but something has happened. The bright light that was inside her has almost gone out.

15

A DYING LIGHT

Grandma and the fishermen and the boy gather round me as I hold Tan. She is pale and grey, and her feathers are burned to stumps.

"What's happening to her, Grandma?" I ask. It is like Tan is disappearing before my eyes.

"I don't know," Grandma admits. "She must have burned out. In the fairy tale it says that when firebirds get old, or use up their flame, they turn to embers and ash."

"Does that mean she's dying?" I ask. Tears fall from my eyes along with the raindrops as I peer down at Tan's tiny fading form.

"I'm afraid so," Grandma says. "But maybe not for good. At the end of the story, the book says that a firebird can rise from the ashes like a phoenix. They can become like new, and in that way they are rumoured to live for ever."

"Will Tan be reborn like that?" I ask.

"I hope so," Grandma replies.

I cup Tan's remains in my hand. All that's left of her now is a pile of ash. As soft as crumbled charcoal. But I don't want to let it go. I don't want to let Tan go. Carefully, I transfer the ash into my dad's empty flask, which is still in my pocket.

*

We take the two fishermen and the boy up to the lighthouse cottage so they can wait out the storm. We get them settled in the kitchen, beside the warm stove. I find them fresh clothes to wear, and Grandma makes them tea and toast. "When the storm's over," she tells them. "I'll row you back to the mainland."

"Thank you," they reply, almost as one.

Soon all three of them and Grandma are laughing together like they've known each other for years. I think the fishermen are just relieved to have survived the storm, and to find themselves alive and warm in a safe place.

I am so busy rushing around I don't hear half of what they're saying. It is only when the young boy smiles and asks me about my bird that I realise how wet and sad and silent I am.

Grandma and the boy and the two fishermen listen as I tell the tale of how I found Tan. When I finish speaking, I open the flask that holds Tan's ashes and peer inside.

I expect to see a glint in the dark interior of the flask. Some sign that Tan is springing back to life. But there is nothing.

"Perhaps if we put her somewhere warm?" the elder fisherman suggests.

We put the flask by the range, close to the fire.

By now the young boy is almost asleep in his seat. Grandma carries him to my parents' bedroom and tucks him into bed there. By the time she returns, the embers in the grate are getting low and threatening to go out. Grandma stokes the fire as best she can and makes another pot of tea for the two fishermen. Then she heads off to the lighthouse to check on the lantern once more. The two fishermen make themselves cosy in their chairs to wait out the rest of the storm. I leave them there and go to bed myself. I am so tired and shocked I can barely stay awake any longer.

The last thing I remember as I close my eyes is Tan's feather lighting up the lighthouse lantern. I wonder if it is still shining?

16

A LITTLE BROTHER

The next morning, the sea is as flat as a pancake, and the air is still and silent. The young boy sleeps in my parents' bedroom long after sunrise, while his father and older brother doze in the armchairs in the sitting room next door. I look in on each of them from time to time. They have slept for so long that it is as if they are in a fairy tale from my book. Some strange version of *Sleeping Beauty*.

Grandma has been out seeing to the hens and milking the goat. She and I have breakfast together in the kitchen. I take the flask of Tan's ashes from beside the range and check it again.

I am hoping that there will be a tiny glow of light inside it this morning.

But my hopes are dashed once again. There is nothing.

"Maybe the kitchen's not the best place for Tan's ashes," Grandma says, "Maybe she needs to be free, floating on the wind."

"Just as she did in life," I say.

I think of the shooting star then. How I saw it streaking across the sky that first night I was alone. It wasn't a shooting star at all, I realise. It was Tan spreading her fiery wings and flying to our island.

"You're right, Grandma," I say at last. "I think Tan needs to fly."

We take the flask and climb the winding steps to the top of the lighthouse.

When we step into the lantern room, there's still a soft glow coming from inside the lantern: the feather.

It is hard to see the feather's light now because of the powerful sunshine flooding the room, but it's most definitely there. I open the lantern and take it out.

The glow from the feather is very faint, but Grandma sees it too.

"I'll get some more oil when I take those fishermen over to the mainland," she says. "Then we won't need to use the feather tonight, Deryn. You should keep it. As a reminder of your friend."

I brush the feather against my cheek. It feels warm. I put it in my pocket.

Grandma and I climb out onto the metal walkway that runs around the outside of the lantern room. Grandma hands me the flask and I unscrew its lid.

"Goodbye, Tan," I say. "And thank you."

I lean over the edge of the rail and pour the ashes out in a cloud of grey dust.

A warm breeze whips the ashes away, and we watch as it carries them far out to sea.

"That wind is special," Grandma says. "It comes from the desert, but people say it carries a little stardust with it. A little magic."

I breathe the warm air. Grandma is right. It does smell faintly of magic.

*

After lunch, the two fishermen and the boy finally wake from their deep slumber and Grandma rows them over to the mainland in her boat.

I find myself alone on the island once more. I sit in Dad's chair in the keeper's office and aim his spyglass out of the window, watching the sea for Grandma's return.

In the late afternoon, she arrives back. She has brought a big barrel of oil with her for the lantern and fresh provisions for the cottage.

"I checked on your mother and father and the baby while I was in town," Grandma tells me as we roll the barrel of oil back to the lighthouse. "I spoke with the midwife too."

"And?" I ask. "How are they? How's the baby?"

"Doing a lot better," Grandma says. "They named him Cyrus, like you suggested, Deryn. He's a bonny lad, full of life. The midwife reckons your mum will need a couple more days to recover. Your dad's decided to stay on with the pair of them. But as soon as your mum's up and about they'll all be back here to join us."

I don't hear half of what Grandma's saying, I'm just relieved that my baby brother is all right. His name is Cyrus, and he's going to be fine!

That night, alone in my room, I put Tan's feather in a jam jar by my bedside. The light from it is very faint, but I can still read my book of fairy tales by it. It's bright enough that when

I want to go to sleep I have to throw a cloth over it. I call it my featherlight. When Cyrus gets home, I am going to show it to him.

*

Two days pass quickly. I go up to the top of the lighthouse tower with Grandma on the day Mum and Dad and Cyrus are due to arrive back, so we can see Dad's boat bringing them across.

I look into the spyglass, staring out to sea. Finally, I catch sight of the sail of Dad's boat. It is weaving its way past the rocks and across the rolling blue water towards the island.

The sun flashes on the boat's sails, making it look as bright as a white cloud.

I can see Mum and Dad together in the boat. Mum has something clasped to her chest. A tiny bundle of blankets. I can just make out a pink face beneath the folds of cloth.

Cyrus. My new baby brother.

I am about to hand the spyglass back to Grandma when I catch sight of something else in the sky. A light.

It is travelling towards us fast, faster than the boat. It's glittering bright orange like it might be a shooting star. But you only see those at night, don't you?

I put the spyglass up to my eye again and stare at the light, squinting against its glowing bright trail.

It's a baby bird, with flaming wings, and it is coming straight towards us. As it gets closer, I recognise the red breast and bright orange crest on its head. It is my firebird. The bird I rescued. The bird who helped us save three fishermen.

Tan. She is coming back for her missing beam of light.

She is coming back for her last, lost feather.

FIREBIRD

LIGHTHOUSE

I am the lighthouse keeper's daughter

And I keep the lighthouse by the water.

Keep the oil lamps burning bright

through the stormy hours of the night.

Keep the trawlers, ships and boats away

from the rocky rocks in Featherstone Bay.

Keep the lighthouse lantern blazing proudly

when lightning crackles and the thunder's rowdy.

I am the lighthouse keeper's one and only daughter

*and with my brother and my firebird I keep the
lighthouse by the water.*

— Deryn Darling, Featherstone Lighthouse,
Featherstone Island, 1907

AUTHOR'S NOTE

The story of Deryn Darling and Tan was partly inspired by two other famous lighthouse keepers' daughters. The first was Grace Darling. The second was Ida Lewis.

Grace was born in 1815. Her father, William Darling, was a lighthouse keeper on the Farne Islands off the coast of Northumberland in England.

In 1838, when Grace was twenty-two, she looked out of the window on a stormy night and spotted a ship that had been wrecked on nearby rocks. Grace and her father rowed out from the lighthouse in their little boat, risking their own lives. They were able to rescue five of the sixty-three people who had been on board the ship. After they had brought those survivors back, Grace's father and two of the passengers went out again and managed to save four more people.

Ida Lewis was born in 1842 in Rhode Island in America. Her father, Captain Hosea Lewis, was the lighthouse keeper at the Lime Rock Lighthouse in Newport. Ida was just twelve years old when she made her first rescue, saving four men whose boat had turned over. When Ida was twenty-seven, she made her most famous rescue, of two soldiers who'd been sailing across the harbour in a snowstorm when their boat capsized.

Both Ida and Grace became famous for their daring rescues. Grace was declared a hero and was known all over England. Ida was called the bravest woman in America. She became the lighthouse keeper at Lime Rock after her parents died of old age.

LIGHTING THE WAY

Lighthouses are important buildings used by sailors to help them find their way and warn them of dangers. For example, rocks hidden under the surface of the sea could sink their ships. They are often built on cliffs, at the entrance to harbours and sometimes on raised stands in the water. Different lighthouses use different flashes and colours of light so that sailors can tell them apart.

Before the first lighthouses were built, sailors out at sea were guided by fires built on hilltops. People realised that if the fires could be built higher up, the light would be seen further away, so they then built fires on platforms and raised them higher and higher.

One of the first lighthouses was the Lighthouse of Alexandria on the island of Pharos built around 280 BC. It was one of the Wonders of the Ancient World before it was destroyed by an earthquake in the fourteenth century.

Lighthouses originally used oil lamps or candles, and the job of a lighthouse keeper was to make sure that all the equipment was working to keep the light shining through the night. Nowadays, lighthouses use electricity and most run without lighthouse keepers. Computer technology is used to light the lamp at dusk and put it out in the morning.

The first lighthouse in the UK was built in Devon in the 1690s to warn sailors off the dangerous Eddystone rocks. There are now over a hundred lighthouses in the UK, though not all of them are still in use.

Our books are tested
for children and young people by
children and young people.

Thanks to everyone who consulted on
a manuscript for their time and effort in
helping us to make our books better
for our readers.